Tyrannosaurus
Max

Jeremy Strong
Illustrated by Lee Cosgrove

OXFORD
UNIVERSITY PRESS

Chapter 1

The trouble with Max was that he looked just like his Dad. They both had wild tufts of hair that seemed to explode from their heads. They both had big spectacles that magnified their eyes. They both looked like mad inventors.

Actually, Max's Dad *was* a mad inventor, so that was OK. But Max just got teased by the Grabbly Gang at school. There were three of them, all brothers, and all bigger than he was. They called him Mad Max, or Fish-Tank, because his eyes seemed to swim behind his glasses. They knew it made him furious and once he even shouted back at them.

'I'll get my big brother onto you!'
The boys burst out laughing.
'You haven't got a big brother! Honestly
Max, you're as crazy as your Dad!' And they
began to chant, 'Max is dotty! Max is potty!'

Max wanted to get back at the gang but, of course, they were bigger than he was. He wished he *did* have a big brother. All his friends had big brothers and they seemed to be very good at sorting things out. He glared at the Grabbly Gang from a safe distance. There was quite a lot of sorting out he would like to do to them.

One day, as soon as Max came home from school his Dad came leaping up the path and pounced on him.

'Max – come and see!' he shouted, and pulled Max into the back garden. 'There! What do you think of *them*?'

Max goggled. His eyebrows went right up and his jaw went right down. Standing in their little garden were two life-sized, shining metal dinosaurs. One had three very pointy horns and powerful, fat legs as thick as tree trunks.

'This is my friend, Triceratops,' said Max's Dad, 'and this is his big brother, Tyrannosaurus Rex!' Dad stood underneath the huge monster and peered out from between its legs. High above him the massive jaws were open wide. Its razor-teeth glinted in the sunlight. And then – Tyrannosaurus moved.

Max screamed as the mighty metal meat-eater snapped its jaws with a loud CLANG of metal teeth. His heart tried to leap out of his body and run away all by itself. His eyes bulged so much they almost smashed out through his spectacles.

'It's OK,' grinned Dad. He reached into the open belly of the beast. 'I just press this button and everything stops.'

The gruesome giant ground to a halt. Max sat down and waited for his heart to stop sounding like ten raving rock-drummers all playing at once. His father seemed very pleased with himself. He stood there with all his hair standing up like an astonished porcupine.

'I've made these for a museum display. Come and look inside.'

Dad lifted Max up so that he could peer inside. The robot was full of motors and cogs and wheels and chains.

'There's the Stop-Start button. Those levers make it go right or left,' explained Dad. 'The big motor drives the legs. It's the same with the triceratops. Pretty good, aren't they? Tell me I'm very clever ...'

'You're very clever,' Max admitted. 'Can I have a go?'

'I thought you'd never ask. You can be
Tyrannosaurus and I shall be Triceratops.
Shall we dance?' They climbed inside the
two creatures and it wasn't long before the
dinosaurs were swaying round the garden,
like two monster ballet dancers from a
strange dream.

It was all great fun, but there was one big
problem. Max and his Dad were blissfully
unaware that they were being sneakily
watched by a very sneaky pair of eyes.

Chapter 2

Binbag had the sneakiest eyes in the street. He and his wife Buster lived just round the corner from Max. Buster and Binbag were robbers. Nobody knew they were robbers of course, because they were very cunning

Buster's tattooed arms bulged with muscles. She got her name from busting into houses. Binbag was very thin and scrawny. After his wife had smashed into a house he would nip inside and stuff all the booty into black bin bags, and that was how he got *his* name.

Binbag leaned out of his bedroom window. He stared at the dancing dinosaurs in Max's back garden.

'Whoopee!' he cried. 'See those robot dinosaurs? Let's steal one!'

'What do you want a robot dinosaur for?' demanded Buster. 'You big baby!'

'We shall use it to break into the jewellery store on the High Street,' said Binbag.

'Brilliant idea!' shouted Buster. 'Have a smackeroo!' And she gave her husband a big, wet kiss.

That night, the robbers crept into Max's garden. Buster sat on top of Triceratops and Binbag climbed inside. He pushed the Stop-Start button and grabbed the levers. Triceratops lurched into action and they went galloping off down the road.

KER-LUMP! KER-LUMP! KER-LUMP

Buster and Binbag made straight for the jewellery store. They aimed their three-horned battering ram at the super-duper-triple-strength-window and charged towards it at top speed.

KERRACKETTY SMASH!

Glass went everywhere. Binbag dashed inside the battered building and stuffed fistfuls of jewels into a sack.

'Tally-ho!' cried Buster, and the robbers jumped back onto Triceratops and went stomping back to Max's house. They parked Triceratops in the garden. Then, just as if nothing had happened, they took their sack of jewels and went off home, whistling all the way.

Chapter 3

The daring robbery made front page headlines. The police couldn't work out how the thieves had managed to break that extra-tough window. The only clues they had were several gigantic footprints, unlike anything they had seen before.

The *Daily Times* carried a photograph of the mysterious footprints. Over breakfast, Max stared at it for a long time. He gazed out at the silent metal dinosaurs standing in the garden.

'Do those footprints remind you of anything?' he asked his mother, who was busily pouring milk onto her husband's cereal and singing, 'One milk bottle, slopping in the bowl ...'

'Yes. We haven't got anything for supper.'

Max wrinkled his nose. 'Why do they remind you that we haven't got any supper?'

'Because they are the same size as empty dinner plates.'

Max groaned and turned to his father, but Max's dad was too busy stirring his soggy cereal and thinking of a way to make it crisp.

Max sighed and set off for school, still staring at the paper. He knew that the photograph was some kind of clue. He took care to avoid going past the Grabbly Gang's house, but they saw him all the same.

'Look,' they laughed. 'Max is going to solve the mystery of the jewel robbery. Watch out, everyone – Detective Inspector Fish-Tank is hot on the trail!'

Max was beginning to think that a giant custard pie catapult would be even better than a big brother.

By the time he went to bed he still hadn't
got to the bottom of the puzzle. He slept
badly, dreaming about dinosaurs wearing
enormous spectacles and ballet frocks. At
half past two his troubled sleep was broken
by strange noises from the garden.

Max pulled on his glasses and peeped out. Two shadowy figures were creeping round Triceratops. Buster grinned at his wife.

'Triceratops makes a brilliant battering ram! That jewellery store was a piece of cake,' he boasted. Max almost fell out of the open window. Of course – those footprints had come from Triceratops! The jewellery thieves had used Dad's triceratops!

'What shall we rob next with these lovely monsters?' giggled Buster.

'Let's go for the big one and break into the bank. Ten-ton Tessie will smash down the walls in no time.'

'Ooh, lovely!' cried Buster. 'Have a smackeroo!'

'Gerroff,' gasped Binbag. 'We've work to
do.' He gave his wife a leg-up onto the beast's
broad back, climbed inside and Triceratops
went clumping off down the road.

Max was in a frenzy. What on earth was he to do? He rushed into his parents' bedroom. 'Mum! Dad! Robbers! Robbers have taken Triceratops and they're going to rob the bank!'

'Doobee-doobee-dah!' squawked Max's mother sleepily, dreaming she was the lead singer in a rock band.

'Dad! Wake up!' panicked Max, pulling at his father's arm.

'Urra-urra,' snored Dad. 'Soggy cereal ... yuck! I shall invent milk that isn't wet. That's it! I shall invent crisp milk!' And he carried on inventing in his dreams.

This was terrible! Max hurtled downstairs and out into the garden. He had to stop those robbers. Max plunged into the garden shed, pulled out his bike and immediately remembered that he had a puncture. He threw the bike to the ground and stared down the dark road in despair.

Chapter 4

Max would have to rouse his parents. He began to run across the garden, and immediately fell flat on his face. He had just tripped over Tyrannosaurus' left foot. Max stared up at the roaring monster. Moonlight glinted on the long teeth.

And that was when it happened, like a sudden shooting star. KAPPOWWW! Max had an incredible idea. He dashed to the kitchen, grabbed a chair and stumbled back outside. He stood on it, pushed open the door in the beast's belly and climbed inside.

Max punched the Stop-Start button and the motors began to hum. He pushed a lever and the jaws snapped shut with a clang. Whoops – wrong one! Max tried not to panic. He had to remember the right levers. He tried again.

Tyrannosaurus lurched forward and began to march across the garden. Max could see the garden fence straight ahead, but this was no time to stop and politely open the gate.

KERRUNCH! Tyrannosaurus crashed through the wooden fence and set off down the road with bits of broken planking clinging to its sides. Max calmed himself. He was in control now and he headed straight for the bank in the High Street.

Tyrannosaurus broke into a bone-jarring trot. There were red traffic lights ahead. Max held his breath and plunged straight through them, right across the path of a police car. Whoops again! Max gulped hard as the night air was shattered by the scream of a siren.

The police car raced up alongside the galloping dinosaur, its blue light flashing eerily. Max went even faster. The police driver was so busy goggling at the dinosaur that he drove straight into a litter bin with a shuddering KER-THUDD! Paper, empty cans, apple cores, banana skins and old crisp packets erupted into the air and came splattering down on the car.

Outside the bank, Triceratops stamped his enormous feet. He lowered his heavy three-horned head and lumbered towards the door of the bank.

KERLUMP KERLUMP KERLUMP KERRASH!

'Do it again!' ordered Buster, and Triceratops smashed into the door once more.

KERRASH-KERRUNCH! The thick wood began to splinter.

'It's almost done!' Buster cried.

For a third time, Triceratops' full weight crashed head first into the door. It burst from its hinges with an ear-splitting crack and toppled to the floor. Binbag jumped out of the beast.

'Oh dear,' he said. 'Look what we've done. We've smashed down the door. Aren't we naughty?'

'*Aren't* we naughty!' giggled Buster.

'We shall be millionaires!' grinned Binbag.

'We shall be *squillionaires*!' Buster shouted. 'Have a smackeroo!' And she gave Binbag the biggest, wettest, slurpiest kiss ever. Binbag grabbed a sack.

'Come on, you daft carrot! We've got a bank to – eeek!' Binbag could only point and gawk, for around the corner came a gigantic rip-roaring, jaw-crunching, fist-punching, teeth-flashing, burglar-bashing Tyrannosaurus rex.

Chapter 5

Tyrannosaurus Max came thundering up
the High Street, just as Buster and Binbag
struggled madly to climb onto Triceratops
and make their escape. The monster
screeched to a halt and loomed over the
two robbers.

'Run for it!' squeaked Binbag, but it was too late. High above them, Tyrannosaurus' huge jaws yawned open and a thunderous voice boomed out.

'There is no escape!' Max's voice echoed and boomed along the dinosaur's long metal throat and out of the gaping mouth.

'Who are you?' trembled Buster. 'We've done nothing. We were just going to take out a bit of pocket money ...'

'Liars!' roared Tyrannosaurus Max. 'Cheats! Robbers! Have a smackeroo!'

With a sweep of his massive head he knocked Triceratops onto its side. Four fat legs paddled away uselessly in mid-air. Buster and Binbag scrambled to escape, but it was quite pointless. Tyrannosaurus Max reached down with his short front arms and grabbed them both. Buster and Binbag twisted and wriggled like a pair of freshly caught fish. Max set off at once for the police station.

Inside the police station a dazed police constable was trying to tell his sergeant that he had almost driven into a Tyrannosaurus rex, but had crashed into a litter bin instead.

'I really did see a tyrannosaurus!' cried the policeman. 'As tall as a house!'

'Yeah, yeah,' muttered the sergeant, 'and I'm Mickey Mouse.'

Just then there was an almighty roar
from outside. The sergeant rushed out
and found himself face to face with a
Tyrannosaurus rex dangling Buster and
Binbag in front of his nose. The door in the
belly opened and Max jumped out.

'Hello,' he grinned at the goggle-eyed
sergeant. 'I've brought you these two thieves.
I caught them robbing the bank.' And he
explained all about Triceratops and the
jewellery store robbery.

Buster and Binbag very quickly found themselves behind bars. Meanwhile, Max climbed back inside the tyrannosaurus and headed towards home. However, he made a little detour on the way.

The tyrannosaurus stopped outside a house that Max knew only too well and usually tried to avoid at all costs. Max knew just which bedroom the Grabbly Gang would be in, and their window was open. How very useful!

Tyrannosaurus Max squeezed his iron-fanged head through the window. The metal mega-monster tapped one of the Grabbly Gang on the head with a sharp claw, then poked and shook the other two boys. All three of them awoke and sat up, wondering what was going on. And then they saw.

'Aaaaaargh! There's a tyrannosaurus in our bedroom! Aaaaaaaaaaargh! Tyrannosaurus attack! We're all going to die! Aaaaaaaaargh!' The Grabbly Boys vanished screaming beneath their covers, like jibbly-jobbly jellies, whilst the tyrannosaurus opened its gigantic jaws and roared.

'Do you know who I am?' bellowed Tyrannosaurus Max.

'Don't eat us!' screeched the three boys.

'I'm Max's big brother. Any more trouble from you three and I will eat you – is that understood? I shall gobble you up like kebabs!' And with that, Max gave an enormous burp. He poked all three boys once again just because it felt so good, pulled his head out of the window and clomped off down the road, giggling.

Max parked the tyrannosaurus in his own back garden and wearily climbed up the stairs. His parents were still fast asleep. Max crawled into bed and lay there for a moment, thinking. Mad Max? Never! Fish-Tank? No way! Tyrannosaurus Max? That would do nicely. He closed his eyes and drifted into a happy, dreamless sleep.

About the author

I was educated with a lot of shouting at schools in London and more quietly at York University. I spent several years teaching in primary schools until I tunnelled my way out with pen and paper. I have married and remarried, acquiring a son and daughter, two step-daughters, five grandchildren and three cats in the process. My hobbies include eating different types of bread and sleeping. I live near Bath.

The idea for this story came to me when I found myself thinking about a boy called Tyrannosaurus Max. What a great name! I have always found dinosaurs to be such exciting, awesome creatures. I also love robots, so why not put them both together? I do hope you enjoy the story because I enjoyed writing it! *Grrrrr*!